Kibitzers and Fools

YOU SHOULD GROW LIKE AN ONION WITH YOUR HEAD IN THE EARTH AND YOUR FEET UP IN THE AIR.

ALL THAT GLITTERS IS NOT GOLD.

OUT OF SIGHT, OUT OF MIND.

IN A PERFECT APPLE YOU CAN ALWAYS FIND A WORM.

CLOTHES CONCEAL THE BLEMISH.

LEND AND BORROW CREATE MUCH SORROW.

UPHILL IS A SLOW CLIMB AND DOWNHILL IS A FAST TUMBLE.

NECESSITY SHARPENS THE MIND.

IF IT DOESN'T WORK, TRY HARDER.

BETTER TO LOSE SOMETHING THAN TO FIND NOTHING.

A WISE MAN KNOWS WHAT HE SAYS AND A FOOL SAYS WHAT HE KNOWS.

IT'S GOOD EVERYWHERE BUT HOME IS BETTER.

WHILE CHILDREN ARE CLEVER, MOST ADULTS STAY CHILDISH.

WHEN THE HEART IS GLAD, THE FEET ARE READY TO DANCE.

A SHLIMAZEL BELIEVES ONLY IN MAZEL.

GOD NEVER TOLD ANYONE TO BE STUPID.

WHAT WE TALK OF BY DAY WE DREAM OF BY NIGHT.

BETTER TO MAKE NOTHING THAN TO MAKE SOMETHING OUT OF NOTHING.

A SHLIMAZEL FALLS ON HIS BACK AND BRUISES HIS NOSE.

A LIAR TELLS A LIE SO OFTEN, HE BELIEVES IT HIMSELF.

WORDS SHOULD BE WEIGHED AND NOT COUNTED.

A STICK HAS TWO ENDS.

DON'T LOOK FOR BARGAINS AND YOU WON'T BE DISAPPOINTED.

IT'S BETTER TO HAVE A GOOD ENEMY THAN A BAD FRIEND.

ASK AND YOU WON'T GET LOST.

ALL IS NOT BUTTER THAT COMES FROM A COW.

IT IS EASIER TO BE A CRITIC THAN AN AUTHOR.

A COW IN THE STALL IS WORTH TWO IN THE FIELD.

A DOG WITHOUT TEETH CAN STILL GNAW A BONE.

KEEP YOUR EYE ON THE BAGEL AND NOT THE HOLE.

WHEREVER THE NEEDLE, THERE THE THREAD.

AN EMPTY WALLET IS ONLY A PIECE OF LEATHER.

FROM THE LOWLY POTATO YOU GET THE CHOICEST LATKE.

WORDS ARE LIKE ARROWS—BOTH DELIVER WITH SPEEDY AIM.

My Aunt Bea always cleaned her home with the same shmatta (rag).

Dedicated to:
The great yiddish storytellers—
Sholem Aleichem,
I.L. Peretz, and
Mendele Mocher S'forim.

My Aunt Gertie ran a kosher chicken market in Brooklyn.

My Uncle Sam played hookey from cheder (religious school).

Uncle Morris was such a kibitzer.

My Uncle Alex sang for his college tuition.

UNITED STATES 2¢

POLSKA 3¢

FIRST CLASS MAIL
To:
Meyer Cohen
19 Rivington St.
New York, NY
U.S.A.

Uncle Harry played the ukulele upside down.

My Mother Toba was a dressmaker in a garment factory.

Kibitzers and Fools

Tales My Zayda Told Me
(Grandfather)

this is my zayda →

He brought these stories to America from his little village in Poland.

Simms Taback

PUFFIN BOOKS

INTRODUCTION

Have you ever called someone a klutz? Or said something was schlock?

Or said yadda yadda when someone was talking too much? Well, you were speaking Yiddish!

Almost all of us speak a little bit of Yiddish now, though we may not know it. Yiddish has become such a part of everyday English that there are some five hundred Yiddish words in the English dictionary.

So what is Yiddish? I like to think that it is like a big pot of soup with a little of this and a little of that thrown in: German dialect mixed with a little French and a little Italian.

Yiddish was the everyday language of the Jewish people who lived in Eastern Europe.

Often their lives were hard, but they struggled on: they sang, they danced, and most of all they told stories.

I've adapted some of these stories for this book and included many Yiddish words with their meanings. Try them out! It may take a little chutzpah (nerve), but don't make it into a megilla (big deal).

Zayn gezundt (Be in good health), enjoy this book, and may you live to be one hundred and twenty.

Simms Taback

The Tales

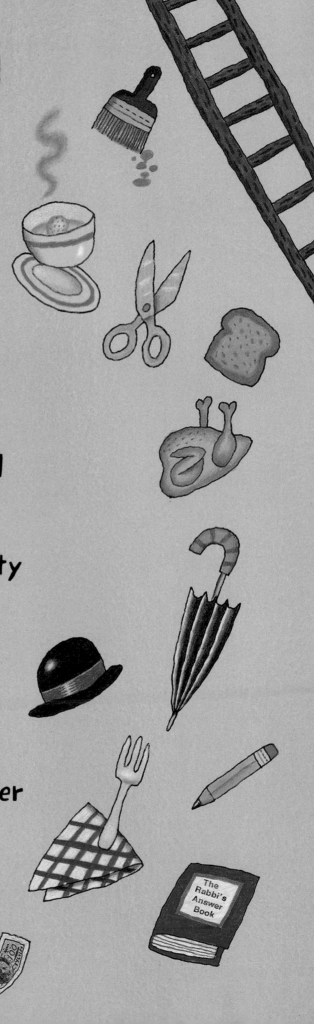

I was playing checkers
with my zayda (grandfather)...

and I suggested how he should move a checker.
"What? Are you a kibitzer?"
he said.

A kibitzer thinks he knows better than you. A kibitzer gives advice that's not very good and that nobody asked for in the first place. A kibitzer is always sticking his nose in other people's business.

The Sign

Motke Rabinowitz, the fish peddler, decided to improve his business. He sold his pushcart and rented a store. He thought, "Why not do a little advertising?" So he painted a sign to hang over the doorway. The sign said FRESH FISH SOLD HERE DAILY.

He had just climbed a ladder to hang the sign, when a kibitzer passed by.

"What kind of cockamamie (mixed up and ridiculous) sign is that?" yelled the kibitzer.

"Why? What's wrong with it?" answered the fishmonger.

"Why say FRESH fish? Would you sell fish that wasn't fresh? Your customers might get suspicious. No?"

"Absolutely right," said the fishmonger. So he painted out the word FRESH and continued hanging the sign.

A second kibitzer came by and yelled up to Rabinowitz.

"Wait! I like your sign, but should

you be saying SOLD? Of course you sell fish. You don't give them away free!"

"Of course," agreed Rabinowitz, and he painted out SOLD.

A third kibitzer came by, complimented him on the sign, and yelled up, "Why do you say HERE? Are you selling fish somewhere else?"

"You're right!" said Rabinowitz, and painted out HERE.
As soon as he had corrected the sign, a fourth kibitzer walked by and yelled up, "Hey! Your sign is a little farblondjet (confused). What do you mean by DAILY? If fish are fresh, they don't come in and go out weekly, do they?"
"I'm in complete agreement!" said Rabinowitz.

He painted out DAILY. Now the sign said only FISH. He came down the ladder and was looking up at the sign, when a fifth kibitzer strolled by.

"Pardon me, Rabinowitz. I don't mean to butt in. But why are you putting up a useless sign that says FISH when you can smell your fish a mile away?"

So Rabinowitz the fish peddler took down the sign. How fortunate he was to get such good advice, he thought.

But that's not the end of the story.

Sometime later, Rabinowitz was sitting in a chair in front of his store, when another kibitzer came by.

"Rabinowitz, it looks like you don't have any customers," he said.

"Business is a little slow," Rabinowitz answered.

"So why don't you hang out a sign?" the kibitzer advised.

A saying:
A kibitzer can be a pain in the neck, but more than one can make you moishe kapoir (all mixed-up)!

A Made-to-Order Suit

Hyman Finkelstein was trying on a made-to-order suit.

"Shnayder (tailor), look at this sleeve!" he yelled. "It's two inches too long."

"Stick out your elbow," said the tailor, "and now it fits just right."

"The collar! It's up around my ears!"

"Stretch your neck and move your head back. See, the collar is now in the right place."

"But the left shoulder is three inches bigger than the right!"

"Bend the shoulder down and they will both look the same. See, now it's a perfect fit."

Hyman Finkelstein left the tailor shop in this awkward position. His elbow stuck out, his head was twisted back so he could hardly see in front of him, and one shoulder was bent all the way down.

"Pardon me, sir," said a stranger. "Would you please tell me the name of your shnayder?"

"Are you meshugge (crazy)?" Finklestein cried out. "Why would anyone want my tailor?"

"Because anyone who could fit a kalikeh (an oddball) like you has to be a genius," said the stranger.

A saying:
A suit of clothing is as good as the tailor.

Chicken Soup

Once there was a poor farmer who was a bit of a shmendrik. This means that he wasn't altogether a fool, but he wasn't too smart either.

The farmer had two chickens. One was healthy, but the other one was sick. He could not stop worrying about the sick chicken.

So he made chicken soup out of the healthy chicken and gave it to the sick one.

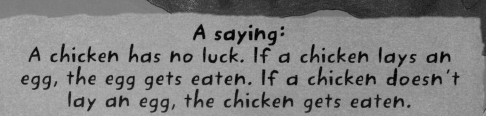

A saying:
A chicken has no luck. If a chicken lays an egg, the egg gets eaten. If a chicken doesn't lay an egg, the chicken gets eaten.

A Philosophical Dispute

Two kibitzers (smart alecs, know-it-alls) got into an argument.

"Since you think you are so klug (smart)," said the first kibitzer, "try to answer this question. Why is it that when a slice of buttered bread falls to the floor, it always lands on the buttered side?"

"You think you are a regular Einstein (Albert Einstein, the famous scientist)," answered the second kibitzer. "I can disprove your theory with a practical experiment."

He buttered a slice of bread and dropped it. It fell to the ground, buttered side up.

"There, you see," he cried. "The bread did not fall with the buttered side down at all. So what about your theory now?"

"Aha!" shouted the first kibitzer. "And you, my friend, think you are an Isaac Newton (referring to another famous scientist)!"

"Paskudnyak (scoundrel)!" yelled the second kibitzer.

"K'nocker (big shot)!" shouted the first.

"Shmendrick (dope)!" yelled the second.

"Klutz (blockhead)!" yelled the first kibitzer. "You buttered the bread on the wrong side."

WRONG SIDE

RIGHT SIDE

A saying: Just because you can talk, it doesn't mean you're making sense.

The Umbrella

Mendel and Itzik, who lived in the same shtetl (village), went out for a walk. One carried an umbrella, the other didn't. Suddenly it started to rain.

"Quick!" said Mendel. "Open your umbrella."

"It won't help," answered Itzik.

"What do you mean? It will keep us dry."

"It's no use. The umbrella is full of holes."

"Then why in heaven did you bring it along?" asked Mendel.

"I didn't think it was going to rain," replied Itzik.

A saying:
Be with a fool and you will suffer the consequences.

An Important Question

   Little Yankel had a question to ask the melamed (elementary school teacher).

   "Melamed, what is life?"

   "I can't answer this question," said the teacher. "I am only a melamed. Go ask the rabbi. He will have an answer."

   Yankel went to see the rabbi. The shammes (the caretaker of the synagogue) led Yankel into the library where the rabbi worked. It was filled with books from the floor to the ceiling. Surely the answer must be here, Yankel thought to himself.

"Rebbe, what is life?" Yankel asked the rabbi.

The rabbi stroked his beard, took off his glasses, and replied, "This is a great question, Yankel. I am only a rabbi of a small village. I do not have an answer to such a question. I would advise you to see the chief rabbi. He is a great wise man who lives high on top of a mountain between this village and the next. They say he talks to God."

So Yankel packed some of his clothing and traveled for two days and two nights until he reached the top of the mountain where the chief rabbi lived. Yankel was surprised to see that the house had only one room. There was only one table, on which lay a very old bible, and one chair. The chief rabbi was in a state of deep meditation while standing on his head. He didn't even look at Yankel when he walked in.

Yankel was scared. This rabbi was a tzadek (a saintly person of great wisdom). But Yankel managed somehow to ask his question.

"What is life?" Yankel asked.

"Narishe boychik (silly boy)," answered the chief rabbi. He remained standing on his head. "Life, of course, is a fountain."

"Life is a fountain?" answered Yankel. "Why is life a fountain?"

The chief rabbi thought about this for a while. He continued to stand on his head.

"OK," he said. "So life is not a fountain."

A saying: A sage can also be half a shlemiel (a fool).

A Shlemiel and a Shlimazel

Once, I asked my zayda (grandfather), "What is the difference between a shlemiel and a shlimazel?"

This was his reply.

"A shlemiel (a fool) will dump a plate of hot soup into the lap of a shlimazel (unlucky person). . . . Farshtayst (Do you understand)?"

Two Brothers

One day, while praying in shul (synagogue), Chaim Meltzer complained to God.

"For years now, I go to shul and pray every day. I study Talmud (all of Jewish teaching) for hours and hours. I observe all the holidays and obey all the rules of Jewish law. Why then, O Lord, do you reward my brother, and not me, with riches, when he is a gonif (a thief) and a no-goodnik (a bum) who has never even seen the inside of a synagogue! And I have gornisht (nothing) . . . only the clothes on my back. Why do you treat me this way?"

After a moment of silence, a voice that seemed to come from nowhere, replied . . . "BECAUSE CHAIM, YOU ARE A NUDNIK (a pest) AND YOU NAG ME TOO MUCH!"

A saying: One's good luck is another's misfortune.

A Case of Mistaken Identity

Hershel ran over to a man he saw in the street. "Labish! Labish Noodleman! How are you? I hardly recognized you. You have changed so much."

"Pardon me, sir," answered the man. "My name is Yankel, not Labish."

"Oy vey (My goodness)! How you have changed," said Hershel. "Even your name has changed."

A saying:
Everyone has his own craziness.

The Caretaker

Shmul Bernstein, a poor shammes (caretaker of a synagogue), opened the synagogue in the morning, swept the floors, straightened the chairs, collected dues, fixed what needed fixing, and closed the building at night. After years of Shmul's being the shammes and never missing a day, the rabbi found out that Shmul could not read or write.

"We cannot have an ignorant shammes in the synagogue," said the rabbi.

Shmul was let go from his job as the shammes. He found a job as a chicken plucker at the local market.

He proved to be a good worker, and clever, too. In time, he saved enough money to open his own kosher (clean) chicken market. Soon he was able to expand his business and buy another market. In the next few years he opened many other small shops in his little village. He employed a tailor, a blacksmith, a bootmaker, and a grocer. Shmul Bernstein was now a wealthy and respected citizen.

He consulted a shadchen (matchmaker) and met the widow Rachel, who had four children. They fell in love and married. Bernstein was now a happy man.

He applied for a loan at the bank to build a new house for his family. On the legal papers, he marked a big X where he was supposed to sign his name.

"Gottenyu (Oh my God)!" said the banker in disbelief. "Are you unable to sign your name?"

"I am illiterate," replied Bernstein.

"How could this be?" exclaimed the banker. "You are so successful, the envy of the entire town. Imagine what could have been if you knew how to read and write!"

"I would have been a poor shammes in a synagogue," answered Shmul Bernstein.

A saying: Everything happens for the better—but there are exceptions.

The Restaurant

"Waiter! Come!" called the customer.

"So . . . I'm here!" said the waiter.

"Taste this soup!" said the customer.

"Twenty-five years we have been making chicken soup," answered the waiter. "Nobody has ever complained—"

"Taste the soup!" interrupted the customer.

"Why? What's the matter?"

"Taste the soup!"

"All right, all right, I'll taste it.... Where's the spoon?"

"Aha!" cried the customer.

der menyu

SPECIALS
Herring
Chopped Liver
Gefilte Fish
+ Horseradish

P   S

A saying: It pays to have a little chutzpah (nerve).

If I Were Rockefeller

"If I were rich like Rockefeller," said a poor melamed (teacher),
"I would be even richer than Rockefeller."
"How can that be?" asked his wife.
"I would do a little teaching on the side!" answered the melamed.

A saying:
Not every thought is
worth expressing.

The Rabbi Is So Smart or How Chelm Got Bigger

Could you imagine a village filled with nebbishers, shmegeges, and shlemiels (jerks, drips, and fools)? The town of Chelm was such a place. Go figure. All the fools lived in one village. And the rabbi, you ask ...well, he was no genius either.

But if you asked a Chelmer (a citizen of Chelm) what he or she thought of the rabbi, you would hear the same refrain.

"The rabbi is so smart. No matter what the question, he always has an answer."

"Rebbe, we have too many he-goats and not enough she-goats. What should we do?"

"Simple," said the rabbi. "Call all the he-goats she-goats and all the she-goats he-goats. Now you have plenty of she-goats."

"Of course, Rebbe, thank you. You are so smart."

"Rebbe, which is more important, the sun or the moon?"

"Certainly the moon," replied the rabbi. "The sun shines only during the day, when it is light anyway."

"Tell me, Rebbe, it's so cold outside. What should I do?"
"Shiver!" answered the rabbi.
"You see how the rebbe is so smart," agreed all the villagers.
In time, Chelm, which was at the foot of a mountain,
became too crowded. There was no room to build even one
more house. Mothers, fathers, grandparents, children, and
grandchildren all lived together in the same house. Sometimes

the cows and the goats lived in the house with them. Soon the chickens had to move in, too.

"Oy vey iz mir (May God help us)," cried the Chelmers.

They were fed up. So the villagers all went together to complain to the rabbi. He would have an answer to this problem.

"Rebbe, the town of Chelm is too crowded and too small.

You can hardly walk without bumping into someone. Our houses are so crowded and noisy. We can't sleep. We can't eat. There is no room even to sit. It is making us meshugge (nuts). What should we do?"

The rabbi thought about this for quite a while. At least until his head started to hurt. Then he had an idea.

"We have to push away the mountain to make more room," he announced.

So the next morning all the people of Chelm gathered in front of the mountain.

"Now, let's all push together," ordered the elders.

The whole town pushed against the mountain. They pushed and pushed for hours. It got to be noon.

It's good to hope but you have to wait.

The Children grow and Chelm shrinks.

If not for the remedy we wouldn't have a problem.

Better to have 10 small worries than one big one!

THE BOOK OF MOST OFTEN ASKED QUESTIONS

The midday sun was hot, and they began to sweat. They removed their jackets and overcoats, laid them on the ground, and continued to push. In the meantime, while the villagers were pushing the mountain, three gonifs (robbers) wandered by and stole all their clothing.

The villagers pushed and pushed until they were exhausted. Eventually, they decided to rest and turned around to see how far they had pushed the mountain. They looked this way and that and could not see where they had put down their jackets and overcoats.

"The rabbi will know where our clothing is," said one of the nebbishers.

"Yes! Yes!" And they all ran to the rabbi and told him what had happened.

"Mazel tov (congratulations)!" exclaimed the rabbi. "You pushed the mountain so far that you can no longer see your clothing."

And that's how the little town of Chelm got bigger.

A saying:
Where there's a will there's a way.

Glossary

cheder (religious school)

Chelmer (a citizen of Chelm)

chutzpah (nerve)

cockamamie (mixed-up and ridiculous)

farblondjet (confused)

farshtayst (to understand)

Gey gezundt! (Go in good health!)

glezzel (a glass)

gonif (thief)

gornisht (nothing)

Gottenyu (Oh, my God!)

Kabbala (Jewish mysticism)

kalikeh (an oddball)

kasha varnishkas (kasha noodle bow ties)

kibitzer (a busybody)

klug (smart)

klutz (a blockhead)

k'nocker (big shot)

kosher (clean, according to
    Jewish dietary law)

matzo ball (a dumpling made
    of matzo meal)

mazel tov (congratulations)

megilla (big deal)

melamed (an elementary school teacher)

menyu (menu)

meshugge (crazy)

meshugener (crazy person)

moishe kapoir (all mixed-up)

narishe boychik (silly boy)

nebbish (a pitiful person)

no-goodnik (a bum)

nudnik (a pest)

Oy vey! (My goodness!)

Oy vey is mir! (May God help us!)

paskudnyak (a scoundrel)

rebbe (a rabbi)

shadchen (a matchmaker)

shammes (caretaker of a synagogue)

shlemiel (a fool)

shlimazel (an unlucky person)

shmegegge (a drip)

shmendrik (a dope)

shmatta (a rag)

shnayder (a tailor)

shnook (a timid shlemiel)

shnorrer (a moocher)

shtetl (a village)

shul (a synagogue)

Talmud (all of Jewish teaching)

tog (day)

velt (the world)

zayda (grandfather)

zhlub (an oaf)

Don't forget to pronounce a like ah, e like eh, and ch like the end of yech!

A SHLIMAZEL FALLS ON HIS BACK AND BRUISES HIS NOSE.

A LIAR TELLS A LIE SO OFTEN, HE BELIEVES IT HIMSELF.

WORDS SHOULD BE WEIGHED AND NOT COUNTED.

A STICK HAS TWO ENDS.

DON'T LOOK FOR BARGAINS AND YOU WON'T BE DISAPPOINTED.

IT'S BETTER TO HAVE A GOOD ENEMY THAN A BAD FRIEND.

ASK AND YOU WON'T GET LOST.

ALL IS NOT BUTTER THAT COMES FROM A COW.

IT IS EASIER TO BE A CRITIC THAN AN AUTHOR.

A COW IN THE STALL IS WORTH TWO IN THE FIELD.

A DOG WITHOUT TEETH CAN STILL GNAW A BONE.

KEEP YOUR EYE ON THE BAGEL AND NOT THE HOLE.

WHEREVER THE NEEDLE, THERE THE THREAD.

AN EMPTY WALLET IS ONLY A PIECE OF LEATHER.

FROM THE LOWLY POTATO YOU GET THE CHOICEST LATKE.

WORDS ARE LIKE ARROWS—BOTH DELIVER WITH SPEEDY AIM.

PUFFIN BOOKS
Published by the Penguin Group
Penguin Young Readers Group, 345 Hudson Street, New York, New York 10014, U.S.A.
Penguin Group (Canada), 90 Eglinton Avenue East, Suite 700, Toronto, Ontario, Canada M4P 2Y3
(a division of Pearson Penguin Canada Inc.)
Penguin Books Ltd, 80 Strand, London WC2R ORL, England
Penguin Ireland, 25 St Stephen's Green, Dublin 2, Ireland (a division of Penguin Books Ltd)
Penguin Group (Australia), 250 Camberwell Road, Camberwell, Victoria 3124, Australia
(a division of Pearson Australia Group Pty Ltd)
Penguin Books India Pvt Ltd, 11 Community Centre, Panchsheel Park, New Delhi - 110 017, India
Penguin Group (NZ), 67 Apollo Drive, Rosedale, North Shore 0632, New Zealand
(a division of Pearson New Zealand Ltd)
Penguin Books (South Africa) (Pty) Ltd, 24 Sturdee Avenue, Rosebank, Johannesburg 2196, South Africa

Registered Offices: Penguin Books Ltd, 80 Strand, London WC2R ORL, England

First published in the United States of America by Viking,
a division of Penguin Young Readers Group, 2005
Published by Puffin Books, a division of Penguin Young Readers Group, 2008

1 3 5 7 9 10 8 6 4 2

Copyright © Simms Taback, 2005

THE LIBRARY OF CONGRESS HAS CATALOGED THE VIKING EDITION AS FOLLOWS:
Taback, Simms.
Kibitzers and fools: tales my zayda (grandfather) told me / Simms Taback.
p.   cm.
Summary: Thirteen brief, illustrated, traditional Jewish tales, each accompanied by an appropriate saying.
ISBN: 978-0-670-05955-3 (hc)
1. Jews—Europe, Eastern—Folklore. 2. Tales—Europe, Eastern.
[1. Jews—Folklore. 2. Folklore—Europe, Eastern.]
I. Title.
PZ8.1.T124Kib 2005 398.2'089'924—dc22 2005003859

Set in Kibitzer regular

Puffin Books ISBN 978-0-14-241065-3

Manufactured in China